Nan's Family

by Anne and Robert (
illustrated by Linda

Open Court Publishing Company
Chicago and Peru, Illinois

On the Mat

Dad sat on the mat.

Pat sat on Dad.

4

Dan sat on Pat.

Nan sat on Dan.

6

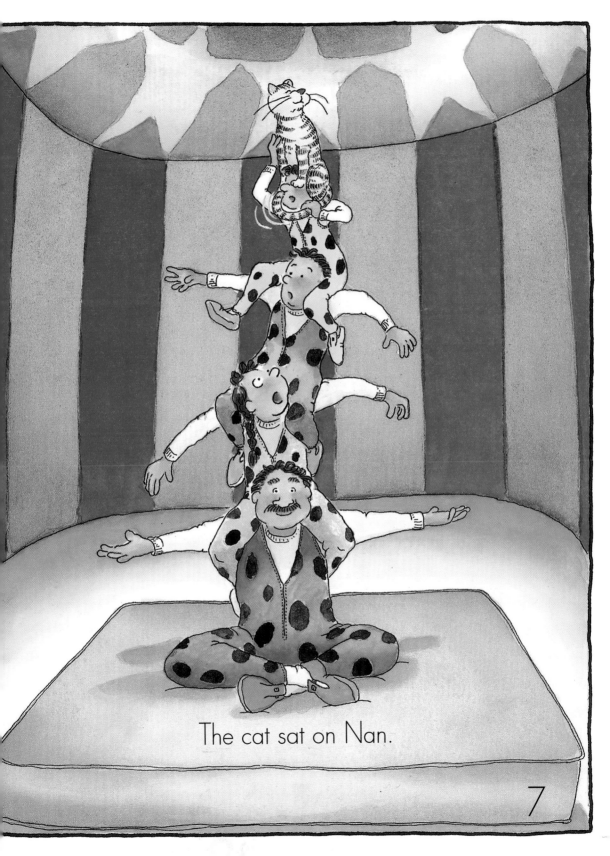

The cat sat on Nan.

8

9

10

The Pans

Dad has a pan.
Dad taps the pan.

Pat taps the pan.

Dan taps the pan.

Nan is sad.

Can Nan tap the pan?